UNDER COVER
A KEITH DANIEL MYSTERY

By

Karen Stevens

Dedication

This book is dedicated to the ladies in green, Lula B Edwards, a beloved aunt and Brenda Joyce Logan Turner Hughes a beloved sister-in-law. Both of these ladies lost the battle with illness the first to a stroke and the second to bone cancer, but they won the war because they are home with our Lord and Savior Jesus the Christ. I will see you again.

Acknowledgment

I would like to thank F. H. Blocker, S. N. Patterson, DJ Patterson II, VZH Hughes, KJ Hughes, V P Hughes, Y R Hughes, and D Patterson for helping me get finished with this book. Without your encouragement I would've stopped writing. Thank you.

Undercover

Prologue

Working together to discover a killer two unlikely people join forces after a chance meeting to get the job done. A Wedding planner who has suffered through three marriages to ruthless, unfaithful men and a divorced detective who has to pose as a gay man in order to trap a killer.

After many years on the job as a beat cop and then a detective and several turns as an undercover agent, Keith is recruited once more to help capture a killer. He finally meets a woman he thinks he can love and is forced to become gay. How does this story end? Let's take a look into the life of a brilliant detective and his pursuit of not only a psychotic killer but a magnificent woman as well.

The killer's name was Brian at least that is what it was this year. He stared in the mirror and tried to remember all of the names he had gone by. All these many years, all because his mother hated him. His reflection revealed a handsome distinguished gentleman. Salt and pepper hair more salt this year but he refused to dye it. Let the years show. Who cared anyway? Shoulders still broad and heavy muscled. Lean hips, trim waist and thighs like tree trunks, thanks to daily visits to a gym

working out so he could win her approval. Who was he kidding

she had been dead for more that fifteen years. He should know

since he was the one who sent her to her grave or at least

scattering those ashes in the back field of their old run-down

back yard.

"John, you get yourself out there and cut that grass. I

don't want snakes crawling up on the porch while I'm sitting out

there." She would shout as soon as I walked in from school.

Where was my snack? Where was my kiss hello like the

other boys complained about getting when they got home from

school? I wish they would stop complaining and spend one day

in my life. They would shut up then. They would be glad to have

a momma who cared enough about them to make a snack ask

them about their day, and kiss them hello. All I got for my

trouble was a smack across the face if I asked for dinner before

she was ready to give it to me. No matter how hungry or tired I

was. Sometimes it might be ten o'clock at night before she would

feed me. If it had not been for the nurse at school giving us the yearly exams and saying I was too skinny for my age. I believe she would have starved me to death.

"John, what type of food does your mother give you for breakfast and dinner? You are about twenty pounds underweight." Nurse Jones said as she pinched my ribs that school day.

"I eat stuff." Was all I could say and I kept my eyes down.

"Look at me", Nurse Jones said.

I raised my eyes slowly and she looked keenly into my face. She begins to write something down and I was shaking because Momma was going to be mad. She did not want anyone coming to her house.

Nurse Jones looked directly at John and said, "Let your mom know that if you don't start putting on weight that she will be reported for abuse." Then she saw the panic there and said, "I will come by and tell her myself. You don't say anything."

After the visit I started getting food for breakfast and lunch but it came with a price. Beatings for every meal. This lasted until I turned thirteen and was bigger than her. The last beating saw me being sent to a foster home. Mom was dead. The police could not figure out how but I knew and I laughed inside the whole while they were investigating the case. Foster care was just an endless stream of homes and more beatings and more killings. After my eighteenth birthday I was released to the world and boy was it freeing.

I always got good grades in school and got a scholarship to the state college and a whole batch of new victims. Who knew smart people could be so stupid?

Now here I am almost sixty years old and still outsmarting the cops and professors and enjoying my life of luxury and killing. I am getting tired of this town. I think I will make a move to a warmer state when it starts getting cold. These people are so gullible. Just because they see me as smart, shy, and successful does not mean there is not a dark side to me. Well I guess they are finding out if the papers are to be believed. I have killed over six people in this city but they are so wrong my actually number is fifteen and counting. Need to beat my Ohio record. I had thirty kills before I left that state.

After casting one more glance into the mirror to make sure that John was totally buried and only Brian, the soft-speaking professor showed he walked out to meet his destiny.

Keith

Keith sat in the standard police issued green visitor's chair with his size 12 feet propped up on the Chief's immaculate desk. As he looked into the silvery gray eyes of the chief he could not but recognize that he was right for the job. His craggy face showed the 31 years that he had been on the job. Not years of sitting behind a desk but actually out there in the trenches with his men. Simms was well over six feet tall although not as tall as me. He carried his weight as muscles not fat. The scar over his right eye was earned when he served in the army and almost took second in a hand to hand fight with the enemy. But that guy is dead and Simms is sitting behind this desk that only had a computer and a picture of his family on it. His two sons and daughter were well past being children. Both sons were following in their Dad's footsteps and joined the force while the daughter followed a different path. She chose to become a lawyer and now acted as liaison to the Department and the DA's office.

Simms draws a deep breath and spits out the words that Keith knew he would not want to hear. "I need you to go undercover as a gay man." Chief Robert Simms said.

"No. No way. I can't do that." Keith says while shaking his head as he drops his feet heavily to the floor and rises from his seat. "You have got to be out of your mind. Do I look like a gay man?"

"Sit down Detective Daniels." Simms says in a deceptively mild voice. "You have to. You are the only one who fits the characteristics of the victims that have been coming up dead. You are 6'5"; well over the 6' height range. You are of the right age although you do not look like it. And you have a very muscular build. All of the basic characteristics needed to pose for this assignment. You also know how to blend into any environment. Come on Keith, I need you on this one buddy."

After taking his seat Keith looks down at his large hands, knowing everything that the Chief said was the truth. During the past three years he had gone undercover on five assignments and played the roles of a crime boss, a school teacher, a fireman, a nerd and a father of nine children. Each assignment had ended in securing convictions for the guys who were destroying their town.

"The Mattapan killer had been running all of the police departments in the area in circles for three months now. Six men had been found dead, all having been openly gay. The only leads on the table were that the victims all had high levels of alcohol in their systems when the autopsy report came back." Chief Simms said.

"It is the conclusion of the joint taskforce that the men have all been at a bar or a club just before being attacked and killed. Every one of the men were between 6"3" and 6"7" in height and over the age of 50. They all appeared to be in good physical shape. The first three were actually members of a gym that was within three blocks of the police station. Two were kayakers and the last one was a member of a swim team that traveled over the state in swim meets." You fit Daniels and you are my best weapon against this killer."

"And who named him or her the Mattapan killer anyway?" Keith asked as he looked at the chief.

"You know the newspapers are always giving names. They had to come up with something and since he or she made the first kill in Mattapan and the last one in Mattapan also they started calling the killer the Mattapan killer."

There was no give in Chief Simms face just an implacable resolve that Keith should and would complete this assignment.

"Ah, you are killing me Chief." Keith said while letting out a big breath. Leaning forward with his elbows resting on his knees the look of disgust on his face is overshadowed by the interest in his eyes. He wants to catch these killers as bad as everyone else. He just does not want to be perceived as a gay man. He had nothing against gays. He just knew that that was not his way of life and never would be. "What if someone who knows me sees me in this disguise? I would never be able to live it down. I am not sure how to act in this role."

Simms remained silent as he watched Keith go through what he needed to get to the point of saying yes. The unbelief, then doubt, then recognition that he would have to do this if he was to actually live in this town in peace.

"It will only be for a little while. Everyone who knows you already know that you don't walk that path and anyone else does not matter." Chief Simms stated with a grim set to his features. "Come on, Keith man, do it for the families that lost their loved ones to this sadistic pompous jerk bag."

"Alright, alright. I will do it. But I am not kissing any guys." Keith says with a serious face as he rises to his feet and walks toward the door.

Chief Simms laughs and says, "Only if you want to. Now go home and look over the reports and wrap your head around this assignment. Once you get into it you will be able to do the fine job that you always have done." Simms stands and looks Keith in the eye as he shakes his hand. "I know you can do this and you know this monster has to be stopped."

Relaxing visibly Keith returns the handshake and responds. "This is just as important as all of the others. I will not let you down. You owe me a cold one when this is over."

"Sure, you want Sprite or Sprite Zero?" Chief Simms smiles. He knows that Keith does not drink alcohol and was actually talking about a Dr. Pepper, his drink of choice.

"You know me so well. See you in the funny papers." Keith could see the lines of stress radiating around the chiefs eyes as he lowered himself into his seat and begin to peck his computer keys. This was serious and deadly.

As Keith walked through the bull pen he heard a few catcalls and stopped at the desk of one of the detectives who made a really racy one. "Now Tom what would you know about that? Have you been fooling all of us and been secretly on the down low?"

Tom's face turned beet red as he sputtered, "Down low. Man my wife would kill me if she thought I was doing something like that."

"Yeah, I know. We all know who wears the pants in your family."

"You are darned right, Mildred runs our home with an iron fist and I am still a happy man. She comes through on all points, if you get my drift." Tom said with a smirk and lifting of his right eyebrow.

The entire room rang with laughter as Keith strolled out

and hit the button for the elevator. He knew every one of the guys had each other's back and could be counted on to do what was needed to get the job done. From the rookie standing at attention in the corner with his brand new uniform on spit shined and creases so pointed you could probably cut yourself on them. All the way to Jim who after 31 successful years, was sitting on less than two weeks before going home to harasses his wife for the rest of her life.

When the elevator button dinged Keith turned to the group and shouted, "Going home to learn to be someone new. Have a great weekend." He smiled until the doors closed then his face turned sour. *What have I gotten myself into this time?"* He thought as he pulled his keys to his 1987 Buick from his pocket. He looked lovingly at his car that was hugely deceptive. There were so many rust spots on it that it was hard to tell if the color was silver or red. But that was the only thing old about the car. It had been rebuilt from the tires up with top of the line everything and when he was in a chase he never lost his man. *Well off to another lonely dull evening. I better stop and get me something to eat.* Driving through the sparse traffic gave Keith time to reflect on his life so far.

***

"What are you going to be when you grow up Keith?" Joey asked as he swung upside down on the monkey bars.

"I'm going to follow in my Dad and Granddad's footsteps and help serve and protect. I know that is the best job for me. Keith responded as he made the last jump shot before grabbing his things. "It's getting late and both of our Moms will skin us alive if we don't beat the streetlight home.

"I'm coming." Joey called as he grabbed his stuff and ambled toward Keith who had already begun walking toward home. "You always knew you would do that I am trying to decide if I am going to medical school for people or animals."

"Now you know that is a hard choice with such different skill sets. You still have about six years to decide. We are just entering middle school."

"Yeah, but you have known what you want to be for the past forever."

"It's in my DNA I can't help but follow in their footsteps. You on the other hand have so many choices to choose from. Your Mom is a nurse, Your Dad is Physical Therapist, your granddad is a farmer, and your grandma is a hairdresser. Keith looked slyly at Joey and said "Perhaps you should be like your grandma: Then took off running.

Joey yelled, "Low blow man." As he sprinted after him.

Rounding the corner the two stopped suddenly gawking at the flashing lights on their street,

"Man that's a lot of flashing lights and they are close to our homes. Let's go." Keith said as he picked up his pace.

Keeping up with Keith Joey said, "Man they look like they are in front of both of our homes. What is going on?"

"I don't know man but I am going to find out. That looks like Sgt. Jackson one of Dad's friends keeping the crowd back. Let's ask him. Keith said as he and Joey squirmed through the crowd of onlookers."

Mrs. Clark spotted the boys and grabbed both of them to halt their progress. She was the meanest lady on the street and both boys had good reason to stop when she grabbed them. She had been the cause of many a punishment because she told everything she saw. But the look on her face was so sympathetic that both boys begin to shake. "Now boys hold up there a minute. You don't want to go in there running like a pack of dogs. Slow down and let me walk with you."

Keith and Joey both looked at her as if she had two heads. "What's going on Mrs. Clark?" Keith asked as he cast glances at Joey and then the flashing lights and back at Mrs. Clark.

"I told Sgt. Jackson I would keep a watch out for you boys and bring you to him when I saw you. I know you always race the streetlight so I knew when you would be coming around that corner. Now stop shaking and get yourselves under control. This is not a time to be little babies."

"We are not babies." Both boys shouted in unison.

"I know, I know that is an unfortunate choice of words. Let's go see Sgt. Jackson." Mrs. Clark actually took both boys hands and walked them the remainder of the way down the block toward the barricades.

As the three marched toward Sgt. Jackson the crowd parted. Everyone was looking but no one said anything to the boys so they were still in suspense about what was going on.

Sgt. Jackson spotted the small group and moved the barricade so they could come through. He looked at both boys with sympathy. Then thanked Mrs. Clark and asked her to step back behind the barricade. As he leaned down to the boy's height, Sgt. Jackson spoke softly, "Boys I want you to listen to what I have to say before you say anything. This is going to be difficult but you both can do this. Keith you are from a cop's family so you know that things go wrong. Joey you've known Keith all your life and you also have known his father and grandfather. So basically both of you know what to expect.

About an hour ago we got a call of a robbery in progress. When Officer Jones arrived on the scene he called three young men running from your home Joey. One of them had a knife and the other had a gun."

Tears started running down Joey's face before he could stop them. He tried to hide his face, and then Officer Jackson said there's nothing wrong with tears. Just listen at what I have to say and then I will take you forward. "Keith, your dad heard the sirens as well as the gunshot and he ran out to determine what was going on. The young man with the gun started shooting. Your dad ducked but not fast enough. Hold on a minute Keith you can't go in right now." Sgt. Jackson said as Keith tried to break his hold.

"Sgt. Jackson, are these two of the children?" Said a detective in a dark blue suit with a notebook and pen in his hand as he walked toward the three. He was tall with broad shoulders and a quick stride. His navy suit coat was unbuttoned and revealed a blindingly white button down collar shirt and a blue tie with red dots. He had a no nonsense look on his face. He too bent down and looked the boys directly in their faces.

"I understand one of you is the son of one of our best police officers. Which one is that?"

"That would be me.", Keith said as he looked up into the detectives face. "This is my best friend Joey; he lives next door to me."

"Hello Joey, you understand when things go wrong is that correct?" The detective asked with a serious expression.

Joey was trembling so badly that he could barely speak so he just nodded his head.

The detective looked at Sgt. Jackson and back at the boys and said let's go over to the squad car. He put his body in between the houses and the boys so they could not see what was going on. The coroner was examining a body on the front lawn and other people were moving in and out of both houses. After installing the boys in the squad car the detective and Sgt. Jackson stood on both sides of the back doors.

Sgt. Jackson spoke first, "Keith and Joey this will began a new chapter in both of your lives. I need you to be strong and understanding. Before we go further I need to know the name address and telephone number of your closest relatives. I'm really referring to the ones who can get here the fastest. Can you do that?"

Both boys looked up at Sgt. Jackson's face and shook their heads up and down indicating they could do that.

Joey spoke first. "My mom's sister lives about 10 minutes from here. Her name is Mary Davis. Her address is 1620 Farmington Rd. Her telephone number is 215-555-1212. But she is usually asleep by now because she works the midnight shift. You may have to call her twice before she will answer."

Keith said, "My brother is probably at the precinct now since he started working at three this evening.

Detective Roberts looked at Keith and suddenly it seemed that the light bulb went on and he knew who his brother was. "So James Daniels is your brother?"

In a trembling voice Keith said, "Yes sir."

Sgt. Jackson said, "I've already called in and he's on his way."

Detective Robert said, "Boys I'm going to call Mrs. Davis and then will wait until James gets here before we go further. Please pray as we wait. I know you boys know how to do that."

The two men stood by the car and detective Roberts called Mrs. Davis. She answered on the first ring since someone had already called and told her that something was going on at her sister's home. Detective Roberts asked her to come to her sister's home as fast as she could. Park about a block up the street and one of the offices will escort you to me."

"I'm on my way out the door. Is my sister okay, what about Joey and his dad. I know Tammy is not there. What is going on?"

"We will discuss it with you when you get here. That will be better. Please drive carefully and safely. Joey needs you."

***

Keith suddenly stepped out of his retrospection. It had been more than 50 years since that night when Joey lost his whole family, father, mother, and twin sisters, and Keith lost his best friend.

He had watched the procedures followed as they investigated the incident. Detective Roberts made a great impression on him. The guy was tough yet gentle. That was his ultimate goal. Although his father and grandfather made great beat cops. Det. Roberts was the man Keith patterned his life after.

Going down that road helped Keith to focus. Do this for Joey wherever he is. I have searched these past years trying to find him but once his aunt took him away after the funeral it was like they left the planet or something. No trace of them anywhere except in my mind.

"Good evening Keith your usual." The short man behind the counter said.

"I don't know maybe I will try something different this time. Let me look at the menu." Keith wasn't sure of his age. Mr. Kim looked like he was a hundred years old but got around his shop like he was fifteen. Close cropped jet black hair surrounded a round face with eyes the color of coal and a nose that looked like it had been broken may years ago. There was always a smile on his face although sometimes it did not reach his eyes. When he gathered the food and stuffed it into the container, the ginger hit your nose first followed quickly by the garlic and onions. Such heavenly smells. I knew I would enjoy this food. "I see you didn't wait. What if I wanted something like your Wonton soup today?"

"Now Keith, you have been coming in here for the past fifteen years and the only thing you get are the garlic chicken and vegetable fried rice. We started your order when you walked into the door. Stop trying to fool me and yourself. That will be ten dollars. Have a nice day." Mr. Kim grabbed the money and moved on to the next customer as Keith laughed and walked out the door with his order.

Fifteen years was a long time.

Keith had been an undercover cop for five years out of the 59 years he has been alive and a policeman for a total of twenty years. He could not remember a time after high school that he had not pursued the crime solving career. His time at university was totally devoted to learning all he could in his criminal justice classes. After graduating from college he married his high school sweetheart and settled down to doing a good job as a bet cop and husband. Things were perfect in the beginning. But after fifteen years of trying to have a baby, with failed attempts, it put a strain on their marriage. So they decided to go their separate ways. After growing up with three sisters and two brothers, Keith always dreamed of having a big family.

They had gone to so many doctors that their health insurance company was threatening to cancel them yet nothing worked. No fault could be found in either of them physically. They were just unable to conceive. The failure turned into arguments and then to just not speaking to each other and finally one day she could not handle it and packed her things and said goodbye. The divorce was anticlimactic and Keith found himself alone in a big house with no wife and no kids after twenty years of marriage. He decided to go undercover after his divorce. His X-wife remarried four years later and adopted two kids and was living a quiet life about 8,000 miles away.

He also needed to get his head wrapped round

what it is he is about to do. Keith noticed a petite woman sitting at a table by herself next to the window. She is wearing a black pin striped pants suit with flats. Her silky black hair is pinned up in a bun. Keith is instantly attracted to her professional look. He walks past her very confidently as he tries to catch her attention. His attempt fails. She did not even blink as he walked past and continued reading the papers in front of her. After Keith orders his food, he tries again to get her attention. She continues to read but Keith can tell by the way she keeps glancing up that she is aware of his interest. Luckily for him all of the tables are filled except the empty chair at her table. Keith pays for his food and although he has a to go bag he walks to her table and takes a chance of not being rejected.

"Is this seat taken?" Keith asks in a very sensual voice.

The woman does not move. She continues staring off into space. Keith tried again.

"Excuse me sweetheart, is anyone sitting here?" Keith asks.

She jumps and looks at Keith. Uh, no. Nobody is sitting here." The woman says in a startled voice.

"I am sorry. I did not mean to scare you." Keith said with sincerity.

"Oh no, It is okay. I am fine." Keith sits down in the seat across from her.

"It looks like you were in deep thought about something."

"Yes, I have a lot on my mind." The woman says looking embarrassed.

"I do not mean to pry, but if you want to talk about it, I am a great listener." Keith tells the woman with a smirk.

The woman looks at Keith as if he said something insulting. But then she smiles.

"I never knew of a man wanting to know a woman's problems." The woman says with the same type of smirk.

"Well, I am no ordinary man." Keith says with a grin. He

stretches out his hand. "My name is Keith Daniels. What is your name?"

The woman stretches out hers to shake Keith's hand. "Hello Keith. My name is Angela Wise."

"It is very nice to meet you Angela. So tell me, what is on your mind?"

Angela looks at Keith as if she can't believe he is for real. "Are you sure you want to do this? Why would I tell a complete stranger what is going on in my life?"

"Well you may not know me now but if we talk you will get to know me. The owner of the place will vouch for me. I have been coming here for the past fifteen years."

"Yes I noticed that you walked in and did not place an order but they prepared your food anyway."

So she had noticed him. Great maybe I am not as bad off

as I expected. "Nothing like having someone knows you so well that they know what you want to eat before placing an order. I live nearby and usually eat here four or five times a week.

"That often. So you must not be a real cook or your wife is very busy."

"No to both of those questions. I don't cook and I don't have a wife. Keith says with a smile. Noticing that she evaded his question.

"I did not ask if you had a wife." Angela says flustered.

"Not directly but…"

"Well yes I guess you would feel that way by what I said."

"Do you live in this neighborhood? Keith asked with a quirk of his left eyebrow.

"I just moved around the corner and my next door

neighbor told me this was a good place to eat and it was also safe."

"Your neighbor was right on both counts. Although it looks as if you have not eaten much of your food."

Angela glances down and then back up into Keith's eyes. You are right. I was starving when I first walked in here. Then I started reading this report and my mind started puzzling out what needed to be done about the facts and time got away from me. My food is cold now."

"Don't worry about it." Keith says as he turns around and shouts. "Hey Mr. Kim can my friend get a fresh order of what she has. This one has gotten cold?"

"Sure Keith, you paying for this one?" Mr. Kim says with a loud laugh.

Someone in the kitchen says with a snicker, "Yeah like

he pays for any of his food."

"Watch it Sam, you are ruining my image with Angela."

"Oh it's Angela now? Hello Angela." Mr. Kim says as he brings her new order out to her.

"Hello, uh Mr. Kim is it?"

"Don't let us spoil this for you we are always messing with Keith. And you can trust him. He is a most worthy person. Enjoy your meal." Mr. Kim said with a wink and a smile.

Keith looked shocked. First Mr. Kim actually vouched for him and second because he actually winked and smiled at Angela.

"You looked surprised. Why is that?" Angela asked.

"Mr. Kim actually winked at you." Keith said as he

turned and watched the small man walk behind the counter. Then turned back to face Angela with that same shocked expression. "I have never known him to wink and smile at someone in all the years I have been coming here."

"He was very nice to me when I came in and explained that I was new in the area and needed to get to know the neighborhood. Perhaps he was just being a good neighbor and letting me know that you could be trusted. Why don't we both eat our food before it gets cold."

Angela and Keith over an hour talking. They talked about their pasts, presents, and what they want for the future. Keith was so involved in their conversation, that he hated his bladder for filling up. "I am sorry. But I need to go to the men's room. I will return."

"Alright. That is fine." Angela says with a hint of sadness.

When Keith comes out of the restroom, he notices that Angela is gone. He rushes out the door to see if he could see her. But, she was nowhere to be found. He sticks his head back in the door and asks Mr. Kim, "Did you notice which way Angela hurried off to?"

"No man, she was sitting there waiting and then I heard her cell phone ring and off she went without even a goodbye."

"Thanks man, well see you in a couple of days." Keith begins to walk home. His mind begins to focus on what he will have to do to get into character to play the role of a gay man. He wants to remove all thoughts of Angela from his mind. She was just a stranger to pass a few hours with. But he knew better than that. They had gotten along so well. He had begun harboring hopes of perhaps asking her for a real date rather than a pick-up in his favorite food place.

***

Angela

The next day, Angela Wise wakes up to the sound of her alarm clock. She had a very vivid dream about Keith. In the dream, she was in a wide field. The field was filled with huge sunflowers, which were blowing very violently because of the wind. But then, out of nowhere, he appeared. He was standing on the opposite side of the field. He had on all white. White pants, a white shirt, and even white shoes. He looked so fine, even from afar. His muscles were popping out of the shirt he had on. When he turned to look at her, the sunflowers suddenly stopped moving. He began to walk towards her. But, before he could make it to her, her alarm went off, waking her up.

"What could that mean?" Angela thinks to herself. *Keith did not strike her as a walk in the fields type of guy. And what*

was with the all-white. Was he her knight in shining armor?

Angela puts the dream behind her, and gets out of bed to get ready for her day. She made quick work of her shower and make-up. No sense in getting too fancy since she would have to do it again around four so she would be in perfect form for the six p.m. wedding. Gray trousers and a crisp white blouse and her trusty flats would do to make the last minute details come together.

Angela rushes from the bathroom as her phone begins to shrill. "Answer the phone Angela." She knew the quirky message could be irritating but she liked it and only turned it off when she was meeting clients or other business matters.

Today was a very important day for Angela. Her most important clients were getting married today and she needed to make sure everything went as planned. Steve and Sydney were both big time executives who gave her an astronomical budget to make their dream wedding possible. They had also been the most cooperative couple she had ever worked for. They met with her on time, made quick decisive decisions and had also given her six more events to plan for their company.

These events would take her out of her comfort zone but would also give her the chance to showcase the skills she had acquired while attending college.

~

Angela has been a well-known wedding planner for over thirty-five years. Ever since she was a little girl, she knew she was going to plan weddings for a living. At the age of eleven, Angela had her wedding planned down to a T. When her college love asked her to marry him, she knew everything would be perfect.

"Angela will you make me the happiest man alive and marry me?" Carson asked as he went down on one knee. His new jeans and polo shirt were a nice contrast to his caramel colored skin.

Eyes wide with excitement and shock Angela stretched out her hand so Carson could put the ring with the tiny diamond on her finger. With a shy smile that turned into a beaming one Angela said, "Yes Carson you have made me the happiest woman on this earth."

But it was far from perfect. Everything that she wanted for the wedding, he disagreed with. That should have been a sign then, not to marry him, but she was in love and brushed those concerns aside. Her parents and close friends also tried to convince her to not go through with the wedding. But nothing could make her believe that Carson was anything other than the kind, considerate guy that he presented himself during the two years that they dated in college.

"Angela, darling why do you allow Carson to talk to you like that? Her mother asked one day after they had attended a tasting lunch for the finger sandwiches that would be served at the wedding.

"What do you mean Mom? Angela asked as she hung up her green pencil skirt that she had paired with a soft cream colored blouse. He was late for a meeting and was upset that Mildred didn't prepare the chicken salad like he wanted it. I am sure he didn't mean to be so abrasive."

"Abrasive is not exactly what I would call what he said to Mildred nor the way he pushed you out of the way when you tried to calm him down." Her Mom said as she sat on the side of the bed in Angela's room.

"He didn't actually push me; he stumbled and fell into me." Angela said defensively as she looked around her room to make sure everything was in its place. All of the perfume bottles were lined up carefully on her dresser. Her picture of Carson sat on her night stand with her ereader next to it. The bold blue curtains hung precisely at floor level covering her window. The family pictures that she had on her chest remained her that her Mom and Dad had a wonderful marriage and that is what she wanted.

"Angela!" Her Mom said quietly.

"He did stumble Mom. Carson loves me and he would never purposely hurt me."

"If you say so dear. I must have missed the stumble and only caught the push."

"Mom you are wrong about Carson and so is Dad. Do you know he said that he was in the deli on Fourth Street and he thought he heard someone who sounded like Carson telling one of his friends that he was going to straighten his new wife out because she thought she was running things? He is the head of the household and his wife would do only what he tells her to do and nothing more or less."

"Yes, Angela he told me and I asked him to speak to you about it."

"Mom he did not see the guy he just overheard him and he thought it was Carson. After all the guy said his new wife. We still have two months before we get married. It could not have been Carson."

"I hope you are right and not making a big mistake. You have always been in love with love."

"Mom, I want the type of marriage that you and Dad have. I know it is not perfect before you say it. But the two of you always manage to work things out. Carson and I will be just like that. We will talk through our differences and come to a mutual agreement just like you and Dad."

"Yes we do. But it is not always easy but we made a commitment to each other that we would honor our vows no matter how hard it was to do so. We also made a commitment to God that we would never go to bed angry with each other."

"That is what I am talking about."

"Angela have you and Carson completed your counseling session with Elder Jones?"

"Not yet, Carson is trying to ensure that he is doing

everything right on his job and he has missed a few. But I have been to all of them and I tell him about them when we get together for lunch on the day after the sessions."

"Carson knows they are important. Don't let him skate by and not attend them."

"He knows Mom and Elder Jones said that if I tell him about the ones he missed and when he gets to the next one he can explain what I told him that would be ok."

"Angela that is not really how the sessions are supposed to be."

"I know Mom, but Carson is new on the job. Cut him some slack please."

"For you I will just encourage him to attend as many as possible."

"Ok Mom I love you." Angela said as she gave her Mom a tight squeeze.

The two women walked to the kitchen, a neat room with gray countertops and black appliances everything in its place. The coffee pot sat directly next to the container with the coffee mugs, sugar packets and creamer which sat next to the mixer and the canisters that held flour, sugar, cornmeal and powdered sugar. There was a small desk situated near the window that held all of the notebooks that Angela kept for each type of event she planned. That was the only area in her entire home that was messy. She was constantly going through magazines and cutting out pictures and putting them into plastic sleeves so that if she wanted to do an event and could use inspiration she had it at her fingertips.

Her Mom looked at the desk and shook her head. "The only thing out of place in the whole house but it looks so much like you."

"Yes that was when I was not trying to be the next B.

Smith. Carson said that organization is the key and it is more peaceful when things are in place at all times. I insisted that this desk would have to be my work area and not to be touched. He agreed and it works out just fine."

Her mother looked at her strangely and opened her mouth to say something then closed it with a frown and walked over to the fridge. "Do you have some water in here or does Carson have a special place for that also?"

"Mom you're doing it again. Yes the water is on the right side of the second shelf. Bring me a bottle also."

"Even in the fridge things are so organized and ridged. Ok I will leave it alone."

The phone started ringing and Angela rushed to answer it. "Hello Carson." She said out of breath.

"Why were you running in the house like a child?"

Carson asked chidingly.

"Mom and I were in the kitchen talking, would you like to say hello to her?"

A long pause occurred before Carson responded. "Sure I would love to speak to your mother but this is not the time. I spoke with Elder Jones today about the next session and he gave me the details. You will need to go without me I have to work tomorrow night." Tell your mom I said hi."

Before Angela could say anything else she heard a click and then the buzz of the phone that indicated he had hung up. She turned to face her mom with a sheepish smile. "Carson said hi but he was at work and couldn't talk."

"What is that look on your face? What did he say now that has you upset?"

"I'm not upset per say just a little concerned."

"Concerned about what?"

"Well Carson said he called Elder Jones and he told him he had to work so Elder Jones told him what tomorrow's session is about."

"That is strange I have never known Tim to do anything like that."

"Me either, you call Elder Jones Tim?"

"Why are you surprised, Tim and I grew up together I only call him Elder Jones in public. Now what does Carson mean he explained the session to him.

"Well he has to work tomorrow and can't attend."

"So he will miss another session. Angela are you sure about this?"

"Mom you have to understand the pressure Carson is under as the new man on his job. Don't look like that he is trying his best."

"If you say so. Well I have to go. Are you coming by the house before your session tomorrow? Chicken and dumplings are on the menu."

"You know those are my favorite comfort food. You are not fooling me Mom I know what you are up to. You just planned to make them after that phone call. Well I love you too and yes I will be there by five. I always take off early on the session days so I don't keep anyone waiting for me."

"You mean Carson waiting for you."

Angela gave her mom that look before saying "Anyone."

"Okay Angela, anyone including Carson. Love you see you tomorrow."

The whirlwind that was her mom was out of the door and Angela was sure she was headed to Head's Grocery right that minute.

The minute they were married he changed. The nightmare of her life was so surreal that the first two beatings had her stunned and believing that he was right and it was her fault. She should have stopped talking when he asked her to. She had been so in love with love that even her own common sense deserted her. Carson was so sorry and presented the persona that he gave her in college after each beating.

The third one left her unconscious and her father found her after trying to reach her for three hours. The divorce happened after three years of this type of abuse. And she did not get into another relationship for over ten years. Her trust meter just did not function and therefore she just refused to try again.

But when she met Dunther at a wedding planner seminar. He was so different. He did not pester her. He would talk with her about the types of weddings he planned and they would meet for lunch or dinner and walk through other ways to make each wedding uniquely tailored to the couples they were planning for.

"Angela how about meeting me for lunch? I have a great idea that I believe will generate money and more events for both of us."

Those were the words that lead her to the first of many lunch meetings. Angela could not tell when they became romantically involved but the subtle manner that Dunther wooed her was something else. "Why don't we attend the next seminar together? That would save gas and wear and tear on our cars." Then, "Let's meet for drinks and discuss the last two weddings."

"That would be great. When and where? Angela said eagerly.

"How about Benny's? I want to try their food for a new gig that I have coming in the next couple of months." Dunther said.

"That sounds like a plan. I have used them before. I can recommend several things you should try." Angela said.

One thing led to another and she found herself married to a bigamist. He was only interested in finding out all of her secrets to her successful business. Within three months of the marriage the truth came out at a wedding that they planned together.

"Dunther Hill, what are you doing here and where is Rachel?" A nice looking older woman asked as Dunther was kissing Angela for the success of the wedding.

Dunther stepped back from Angela as he recognized the voice of his mother-in-law.

"Who is this floosy?" She asked with righteous indignation.

"Excuse me, just who are you and why are you speaking

to Dunther like that?" Angela said in outrage.

"Listen you may have planned a wonderful wedding but this is between my son-in-law and myself. You may excuse yourself." Mrs. Anthony said.

"Your son-in-law. Dunther what does this mean. You never told me you had been married before."

Before, what is she talking about Dunther? And why are you here and not in Arizona attending that conference Rachel said you were attending?" Mrs. Anthony said.

"What is going on here Dunther?" both women asked at the same time.

"Please ladies; let's discuss this somewhere more private everyone is starting to stare at us."

Dunther lead both women into the small office of the reception hall and sat down heavily into as metal chair as Angela and Ethel took the two cushioned chairs and stared at him pointedly.

Angela cleared her throat and stated, "Explain now and no lies."

"Angela, I am truly sorry." Dunther said with regret in his voice.

"That is not an explanation, I am waiting for what is really going on here and it had better come quickly." Mrs. Anthony said.

***

Her heart was broken and she believed she would never find love again. Then Shawn came into the picture. He was perfect. But so was Dunther, so she thought. Shawn knew of her past two marriages and tried to show Angela that he was different, that he was not like them. But Angela would not let him. She was so broken that she did not know how to trust a man. She let her insecurities and past relationships ruin the marriage she had with Shawn. He could not deal with her always asking where he was at, who he was talking to, and being scared every time he moved suddenly around her. So he asked her for a divorce. Angela was devastated and swore she would never marry again or even let another man get close to her. In her mind, she was a 62-year-old failure.

The wedding Angela coordinated was a success. Everything went according as planned. The bride looked beautiful, the venue was gorgeous, and the reception was phenomenal. Now it was time for her ritual that she does every time she completes a successful wedding. She would always go to Mistral and treat herself to the grilled beef tenderloin, sautéed spinach with garlic, and her favorite dessert, warm chocolate torte with vanilla ice cream. She would go at least three times a month. The waiters even knew her by name.

"Hello Ms. Wise. The usual?" The hostess asked Angela as she walked in.

"Yes, the usual Mary. How have you been?" Angela asks.

"I am well. Thank you for asking. I see you had another great wedding today."

"Yes. It was fantastic." Angela says with joy in her voice.

"That is wonderful. Well here is your table. Enjoy." The hostess says before walking away.

While Angela is waiting for the waiter to come, she looks up and sees him. The man from last night, Keith, the one that was in her dream. He was sitting at a table with another man and they were holding hands.

"He is gay!" Angela says to herself.

The reason Angela left last night, without telling Keith goodbye, was because she felt a connection with him. But she did not want to act on it because, in her heart, she knew it would only lead to heartbreak. But looking at Keith hold hands with another man, makes her feel silly for even thinking there was anything between them.

Keith spots Angela staring at him, and looks shocked. He is on a "date" with the potential serial killer. He cannot blow his cover. But the look in her eyes is letting him know that she thinks he is gay. He tries to think of something quick.

"I need to go to restroom baby." He tells his date.

Keith gets up out of his chair and walks toward Angela. As he passes her he whispers, "Follow me". Angela hears him and looks back to see where Keith was going. She notices that he is going towards the restrooms. Angela debates if she really wanted to follow him or not, but decides to go. When Angela turns the corner to get to the restrooms, she sees Keith standing along the wall. He grabs her hand and leads her to the door leading to the back alley garbage cans.

"Where are we going Keith?" Angela asks nervously.

"I have to tell you something, but nobody can hear."
When they get outside, Keith faces Angela towards him.

"I am not gay." He says with a straight face.

"Then what are you doing here? Why are you holding
another man's hands, like you are a couple?"

"I cannot tell you. But just believe me when I say that I
am a hundred percent not gay. You just need to trust me." Keith
says pleading with Angela.

When Angela hears Keith say the words "trust
me", she cringes up. How could she trust someone she barely
knew? "I, I can't." Angela quickly hurries away.

When Keith comes back inside the restaurant he
passes by Angela's table and sits back in his sit. He glances over

at her, but she has her head down, trying not to look in his direction. Keith continues his dinner with the possible suspect named Brian Spence.

"I am so glad you messaged me. You are so handsome." Brian tells Keith.

"Oh, I just knew if I would not have written you the message, that my life would be incomplete if you were not in it." Keith says while gaging on the inside.

"Oh how sweet. Did you want to order dessert?" Brian asks Keith.

"No, I would rather have dessert at my place." Keith says while winking and smiling hard.

"Ooh, as much as that offer sounds good, I think we need to take it slow. How about we see each other again tomorrow night? I could cook for you." Brian says.

Keith knew he had to say yes. He was getting closer and closer to Brian trying to make a move. "That sounds like a plan."

This time Brian excuses himself to go to the restroom. While he is gone Keith writes his number on a napkin. He then calls the waitress over.

"Can you please give this to the woman sitting over there?" Keith says while pointing to Angela.

"Ah, you mean Ms. Wise. Yes, I sure can."

"Thank you." Keith says. Keith watches as the waitress hands Angela the napkin. She looks up at Keith in confusion. He then mouths the words, "Please call me tonight." Angela nods in agreement even though she still contemplates really calling him. When Brian gets back from the restroom, he and Keith pay for their meals and then head out of the restaurant. Angela watches as Keith and Brian leave holding each other's hands.

When Keith gets home, he calls the Chief as soon as he enters the door. Walking toward the kitchen he notices that it is looking a little scruffy and starts putting things away as the phone rings.

"Hello Daniels, I hope you have a good report to give. It is getting closer to the striking time and I don't want another murder on the books if we can stop it from happening." Chief Simms says in that rumbling voice that always sounds like he is chewing on rocks.

"I believe I have him hooked. The way he gets his marks targeted is to simply invite them to dinner then set up another date where he cooks for them. I am to meet him at his place tomorrow night. The address he gave me is one of those efficiency apartment complexes near the gay community hangouts area."

"That fits in with the established pattern. I believe we will end this sooner than we expected. You get some sleep and we will get things set up tomorrow. Task meeting is at 11 a.m. sharp."

"Chief one more thing we need to check into overnight. Get the tech guys to dig deeper into that website called Date.com. Brian said he met his last "friend" on that site but it did not last. He indicated he had been on the site for almost three years. You know my first contact was through the site. Perhaps there is a connection there that may lead to other victims."

"Right I will give them a heads up and perhaps they will have something else to share in the morning. Good night Keith, Good work." The line went dead before Keith could say anything else.

The next two hours saw Keith cleaning not only the kitchen but the den and both bathrooms. He could not believe he was doing that but he knew he was waiting on that call. *She has to call I know what she saw but we had a connection at Mr. Kim's shop. Why am I so obsessed with the lovely Ms. Wise?*

Yeah, I know she took my breath away and now I can't get her

out of my mind. Please Angela call me.

Angela

Angela grabbed a cab and got home within fifteen minutes. The ride seemed endless.

"You okay miss? You look like somebody stole your dog and left you with a note saying got you." The cab driver said as he barreled through a yellow light.

"I'm fine." Angela said then looked into the drivers eyes, "Left me a note saying got you."

"Yes, I was trying to make you smile you seem so

down." said the driver.

Angela gave him a small smile then looked back at her hands and mumbled. "I'm fine it has just been a long and trying day. So many things happening that I did not expect. Thanks for trying to make me feel better. I added something extra for your kindness. Thanks for the ride"

Angela scrambled out of the cab and ran up the steps to her apartment. She glanced over her shoulder before entering and was surprised that the cabbie sat and waited until she got inside before pulling away. *"Well there are still some gentlemen in this city. I wonder if Keith is one of them. Perhaps he is on the down low. If that is the case then I want nothing to do with him. Get out of my head Keith. I have a life that I like and am comfortable. I don't need a man to complicate it. Especially not a man who could swing for both teams."*

Angela laid her keys and purse on the hall table and scurried down the hall to put on a pot of tea before showering and getting ready for bed. The kitchen was tiny and it did not take long for the kettle to sing and the tea was soon ready with just a packet of stevia. She had long since replaced her three teaspoons of sugar with the stevia packet. It made the tea sweeter without taking away the taste of the soothing oolong tea.

After showering and rubbing down with moisturizer Angela crawled into bed and kept looking at the note and the number.

Angela did not want to get in the middle of Keith and his male love interest. She felt that it would be too complicated to try to get to know Keith better. What she saw tonight was a big turn off. But she did enjoy their conversation in the neighborhood restaurant. She always heard gay men were the best friends to have. So she decided to call Keith, just to be friends. When she dialed the number, Keith answered on the first ring.

"Hello." Keith answered quickly.

"Hi. Is this Keith?" Angela asked, knowing it was Keith.

"Yes. This is Angela, right?"

"Yes. Hi." Angela says nervously. "Before you say anything, I just want you to know that I do not judge you for being gay. I mean, at first, I was really attracted to you. That is why I left. I did not want to get too involved. But after seeing you tonight, holding hands with that man, I just felt so stupid. Of course someone as attractive as you would not be into someone like me."

"Whoa. Slow down honey. First of all, I am not gay. Secondly, I could lose my job for telling you this. There are some things about me that I really want to tell you and I just feel we have this connection that seems so right." Keith said with a faint tremor in his voice.

"Yes, I felt it also but after seeing you holding that guys

hand I felt that I must be mistaken. There is no way that type of feeling could be coming from a gay man."

"You have to believe me that well okay here goes. But you have to promise to keep it extremely quiet. There are many lives at stake if you were to repeat anything I say to you tonight. Do you understand?"

"Keith, you are scaring me. What is going on that involves taking people's lives? Are you with the CIA, FBI, Homeland Security."

"Hey hold on baby. You are throwing things out so fast that I can't get a word in edgewise. You are partly right but I am an undercover cop."

"Undercover cop? You mean to say that you don't really look like you do? You mean to tell me that what you are only five feet ten and are wearing lifts in your shoes? Is that really your face or is that make-up. I mean not that I am into judging people by their image but well you know the first thing I noticed about you was how tall you were and how hand." Angela let that trail off and let out a long sign. "Well you know what I mean."

"Yes, I know what you mean but you are letting your imagination and the stories you see on TV get to you. Keith laughed loudly, lifts in my shoes. My Mom and Dad would be horrified if they even thought I would do something like that. No I am six feet six inches tall. My Mom was six feet and my Dad was six seven. I am playing gay in order to catch the Mattapan Killer. And thirdly, you are a very beautiful woman, and I would be a fool not to be attracted to you." Keith said in a rush.

Angela began to blush over the phone. She was propped up in her frilly bed with three of the many pillows that she had behind her back. The room was lit by only a small alarm clock and the moonlight filtering through the blinds. As Angela looked around the room she wondered if Keith would look strange in this room. The bed was certainly large enough since it was a king sized bed. When she bought it she fell in love with the thing. Tall spires sticking out of each bed post and heavy. It had taken two men carrying each section to get it into the room. Yet it looked like it belonged here. The dresser and chest were equally impressive although the dainty perfume bottles adorning the dresser may not be his style. The dresser sat beneath a window and a small sliver of the moon shone through the burgundy drapes that were closed for the night. The little corner reading nook filled with two overstuffed chairs and a small table seemed like her one indulgence toward what could be considered man cave material. They seemed like wishful thinking when she bought them but she could now see the two of them sitting there discussing their day until time for bed and another restful night.

"I have been following the story on the news. There have been six men killed so far. They all look buff like you. Are you telling me those gorgeous men were all gay?" Angela said with surprise.

"Yes they were all gay. So you think I am buff and gorgeous?" Keith said.

"You stop Keith, you look in the mirror every day and you know what you see. How often do you go to the gym?"

"Well I try to hit the gym every day except Sunday. Church takes up my morning and then resting and getting ready for the next week fill up the rest of the day."

"Which church do you attend? I have been visiting churches that are walking distance from the apartment but have not settled on one yet."

"I attend St. Luke about two blocks up from Mr. Kim's on the left side of the road."

"I have been to that one. The minister was very nice and he invited me to attend Bible Study also. They have a day and evening Bible Study."

"I know. Rev. Alexander always reminds me that

whatever shift I work I will not miss anything. He covers the same material day and evening. I have attended both sessions. He does a great job of explaining God's Word. So you are a believer?"

"Yes, I was baptized when I was around nineteen. When did it happen for you?"

"I was baptized when I was eleven but I did not truly develop a personal relationship until after my divorce. I was just doing lip service to my faith. Keith and Angela talked all night until five o'clock in the morning. They talked about everything they missed the first night they met.

Keith

Later on that day, Keith had backup waiting at Brian's house for his signal. He was wired to a microphone and ready to catch this maniac. When Keith knocked on Brian's door, Brian answered wearing a red and gold silky robe and the thong to match. Keith was caught off guard, and gasped when Brian opened the door. He tried to play it off.

"My, don't you look good enough to eat." Keith said, praying he would not laugh and blow his cover.

"Hey baby. This is all for you." Brian said.

When Keith walked through the door he noticed Brian holding something behind his back.

"What are you hiding?" He asked nervously. The squad

downstairs heard the change in Keith's voice and got ready to attack.

"Come in and I will show you." Brian says.

The moment Keith hears him close the door to the apartment, Brian grabs him from behind. He then takes the machete he was holding in his hand and puts it on Keith's neck. The team downstairs hears and begins to make their way upstairs. Keith bends down and kicks Brian in the groin. Brian falls to the floor with pain, dropping the weapon at the same time. Keith sees that and runs and tries to grab it. But Brian notices and grabs it before he could get to it and swings and slices Keith's arm and shoulder. That is when the SWAT team breaks the door down and seizes Brian, and handcuffs him. Keith is bleeding uncontrollably and he blacks out and collapses.

"Get him out of here," Sgt. Jackson yells as Brian turns around and spits on Keith.

Two of the unit members remove him none too gently and suddenly a loud thunk happens.

"Sorry about that man I didn't see the door." is heard above the cursing coming from Brian.

"Police harassment." Are the next words that float up the stairs then silence after the sound of a loud crash as if someone had been run into a wall.

Chief Simms walks in with the forensic team on his heels. "I want the whole place processed. Don't miss anything. You are looking for any and all things. Nothing is too trivial. It could lead to the identity of his other victims."

"Yes sir, we are on it sir." One of the newer technicians responds as the others set out their equipment and begin photographing and cataloging the room.

"Chief Simms you have to see this." a growly voice comes from the other room says.

"Give me a second." Chief Simms leans over Keith who has been strapped to a gurney. "You did well tonight. He never suspected a thing. You follow the doctors' orders and when you awaken I think you will enjoy your surprise."

"Ok, let's see what you got." Chief Simms says as he strides purposefully down the hall toward a room in the back. He enters what appears to be a regular bedroom. Double bed with a meticulously made cover, a dresses that is perfectly arranged with a comb, brush and mirror as well as a chest of drawers that have a set of shaving utensils sitting in the very center. The curtains are drawn but not tightly.

"Back here Chief." The growly voice says and the chief rounds the corner to find a concealed room and Jeff Lipton the chief forensic tech sitting in front of a computer. "We have it all here and I can tell you now that it is far worse than we expected. He kept meticulous records. We will be able to put a lot of minds at rest when we finish with this."

The man kept talking but Chief Simms was not listening he was going from picture to picture. There were hundreds of them and each was either circled or had a heart drawn around them. As he traveled around the room he noticed that each set of pictures were grouped by states. The two he found the most interesting were the only woman who had a heart, circle and black X over her picture and the one of Keith who had a heart and the word final written on his face. "Stop a minute Jeff and get a good picture of this for Keith. He is honored as the final one. Little did Brian know how true that statement was?"

"Got you!" Jeff said with an excitement the Chief was not used to hearing from the taciturn man. "I found the mother lode. He has been using Date.com all over the country. Oh my God. Chief you are not going to believe this. He has hit every state in the continental US. Wait no he has hit every state. Hawaii and Alaska have their own special section. We will be working through this for weeks, months even to find out how many men he has destroyed."

Chief Simms leaned over Jeff's shoulder and watched as he clicked through what appeared to be a detailed spreadsheet of what could only be termed a kill sheet. Dates, states, cities, restaurants, even the names of the men's families were listed. No address but there was enough data to start locating the men's families. "Just when you think things could not get any worse they do. I will set up a meeting in the morning. Do what you can tonight and secure everything. Follow procedure to the letter. We don't want him getting away on a technicality. Once you have the data and equipment stored write me up a report and go home. I can see a lot of long nights and days ahead. Good work Jeff."

As the chief walked through the rooms he glanced into another bed room and there were more pictures on the wall. "Timothy come process this room. Be very detailed and secure everything by the book no shortcuts. By the book, you understand no slipups. We have a lot of families wondering what happened to their loved ones and we have to give them closure.

Epilogue

When Keith finally wakes up, he is sitting in a hospital bed with an IV hooked to his arm. Angela is asleep sitting in the chair next to his bed. Before he went out to go to Brian's house, he had called the chief and gave him Angela's number. He told him to call incase anything was to happen. That is exactly what he did.

"Angela? Mm. Ouch. Angela?" He calls out. Angela opens her eyes immediately and jumps out of her chair and goes closer to Keith.

"You are awake. How are you feeling?" Angela asks concerned.

"I am feeling okay. Just a little sore. I am glad to see you though." Keith says with a grin. "I was not sure if Chief Simms would call you. You look beautiful."

Angela blushes. "I was worried. When Chief Simms called me, I thought you were dead. I was so scared." Angela begins fussing with the sheets and glancing at Keith then her eyes would dart away. He sounded so gruff and then he sent a detective to pick me up and escort me to your room."

"Oh you were worried, huh? So that means you have some sort of feelings for me then?" Keith says with a smirk as he moves his arm and ends with an expletive.

Angela smiles. "No. I was just mad you did not get to buy me dinner first. Are you okay? Does it hurt to move that arm?" Angela and Keith, both, begin to laugh.

"Hurts a bit." Keith says as he turns his head to look at the IV attached to his arm. "It would feel better if you gave it a kiss."

"So you think that one of my kisses will help heal an arm that was almost sliced off." Angela says as she smiles down into Keith's eyes.

"Well it may not make my arm feel better but it sure will make me feel better." Keith said with a wink.

"Well here's to making you feel better." Angela leaned down and planted a soft featherlike kiss on Keith's lips and pulled away.

"I feel better already. Let's find that doctor and get me released" Keith said as his eyes slowly closed.

Angela watched him with undisguised amusement and settle into her chair to watch Keith sleep. Hours later they were both awaken by whispered voices in the room. Angela looked into the worried gaze of Chief Simms and three other officers.

One of whom was the one who brought her to the hospital.

"Hello Ms. Wise. I am Chief Simms and these two with me are Sgt. Jackson and Detective Cooper, you already know Detective Denton." Chief Simms said as he walked over and shook her hand.

"Hello to each of you." Angela said as they shook her hand. "And again thank you for calling and thank you for bringing me. He has been drifting in and out of sleep for the past four hours. The doctor was in about five" Her speech was interrupted by a knock on the door and the doctor's entrance.

"Well I see we have a full house. Hello Simms checking up on your super hero?" Doctor Watson said as he pulled his stethoscope from his pocket and begins checking Keith's vitals.

This action brought Keith awake and he grinned at his visitors. "Not dead yet Denton but I believe you can have my assignments for a while."

A loud laugh erupted from Detective Denton's mouth before he said. "No way, your assignment should come with hazard duty pay. What is this your fifth hospital stay in five years. I think I will stick to my jewelry store break-ins thank you very much."

That was the beginning of the rest of their lives. Angela and Keith married four months later. They both agreed that waiting would not make any difference. She was able to have the dream wedding she always wanted. Because Angela was well over her childbearing years, she and Keith decided to adopt. They adopted a ten-week-old St. Bernard puppy. Keith was content with that. Angela was able to get past her insecurities and embraced her relationship with Keith. She figured she was not getting any younger, so why not try love again. This time was the last and best marriage she could ever have dreamed of.

About the Author

Karen has been a reader from the age of 4. For her young adult life, she would can always be seen with a book or asking someone to read to her. She began to write stories in the first grade and has not stopped writing since. She has ventured in many different arenas in her life before finally settling on writing short stories after retiring from 37 years in the public school system. She has traveled extensively throughout the continent of North America. You may friend her on Facebook. She writes under the name Marier Farley as well

She has several other eBooks as well as several other books that are coming out soon.

http://www.amazon.com/To-Love-Wisely-Not-All-ebook/dp/B00IY3GPEA?ie=UTF8&*Version*=1&*entries*=0

http://www.amazon.com/Twice-Shy-Love-Wisely-Book-ebook/dp/B00KPHGJDK?ie=UTF8&*Version*=1&*entries*=0

http://www.amazon.com/They-Knew-How-To-Cook-ebook/dp/B00N137WIG?ie=UTF8&*Version*=1&*entries*=0

http://www.amazon.com/Stranger-Town-Love-Wisely-Book-ebook/dp/B00IEKB4EY?ie=UTF8&*Version*=1&*entries*=0

www.amazon.com/dp/B01I8EO8XO#navbar

The Ladies In Green https://www.amazon.com/dp/B01I76IJBU#navbar

It's Time to Move http://tinyurl.com/jflob89

Praying Prayers of Accountability http://tinyurl.com/zp7g3sa

Praying the Promises of God http://tinyurl.com/gvclmy4

Praying Prayers of Encouragement http://tinyurl.com/zzvgmoa

Prayers of Gratitude http://tinyurl.com/z3barsa

Prayer Changes Things http://tinyurl.com/h8lh6mg

Prayers For Relationship Building http://tinyurl.com/hw3alss

12981117R00049

Made in the USA
Middletown, DE
24 November 2018